# Roberto Piumini

# Glowrushes

Translated from the Italian
by Leah Janeczko

Pushkin Children's

Pushkin Press
65-69 Shelton Street
London WC2H 9HE

Original text © 1993, Edizioni EL S.r.l., Trieste Italy
English translation © Leah Janeczko 2022

The right of Leah Janeczko to be identified as the translator
of this Work has been asserted by them in accordance
with the Copyright, Designs & Patents Act 1988

*Glowrushes* was first published as *Lo Stralisco* by
Giulio Einaudi editore S.p.A. in Turin, 1987

First published by Pushkin Press in 2022

This book has been translated thanks to a contribution awarded by the
Italian Ministry of Foreign Affairs and International Cooperation

Questo libro è stato tradotto grazie a un contributo per
la traduzione assegnato dal Ministero degli Affari Esteri
e della Cooperazione Internazionale italiano

1 3 5 7 9 8 6 4 2

ISBN 13: 978-1-78269-381-9

Designed and typeset by Tetragon, London
Printed and bound by Clays Ltd, Elcograf S.p.A.

www.pushkinpress.com

To my son Michele,

who gives me the idea of love

In the Turkish city of Malatya lived a painter named Sakumat, who was neither young nor even old. He was the age at which wise men know how to be their own friend without risking their friendships with others.

Though the rocky valley of Malatya didn't shine with great beauty, Sakumat painted wonderful landscapes and invented others, arranging shapes and colours just as—had they been real—a fine Creator would have done.

Many wealthy cattle owners, horse traders and textile merchants would summon Sakumat to their homes to have him embellish a corner, the back of a portico, or broaden the light on a windowsill by painting his colourful flowers. Yet even if no one had requested his artwork, Sakumat would have painted all the same, because to him brushes were like fingers and with each brushstroke he tenderly offered a drop of his life's blood.

As for the landscapes he imagined, who knows where he'd seen them. Not even he knew. Perhaps they didn't exist anywhere in the world or in any human dream. Yet looking at them, they were like real lands that one could smell and touch. The more a person looked at them, the more their body would slip away through their eyes and journey, whole and alive, to colourful realms full of peace.

One day a big, strong man knocked on Sakumat's door. He wore a low turban typical of the valleys to the north of Malatya. "You are Sakumat, the painter?" he asked.

"And this is my home, man from the mountains. Who are you? And why have you come looking for me?"

"I am Kumdy, sceptre-bearer of the burban, Ganuan, lord of the land of Nactumal. On his command I have come to ask that you travel

to our valley, to his palace, because he wishes to speak with you and commission from you a painting."

Sakumat had never been to the northern valleys, but he had heard of them. He knew they were rugged, secluded lands, so he replied that he was very busy and could not accept the honour of the invitation.

"Ganuan, my lord the burban," the emissary said, "imagined you would find the journey inconvenient. He gives you a gift of the horse you see tied to mine and wishes me to say that the work he would like to entrust to you is of great value, and just as great will be your payment."

His eyes delighting in the beauty of the horse that pawed the ground behind the messenger, Sakumat reflected. More than the burban's generosity and the promise of riches, he was curious as to why one of the proud, powerful lords of the mountains would insist in such a manner and tone. And so he objected no further, telling the messenger he wouldn't accept the horse, since he had one that was old yet could still handle the journey. Then he asked Kumdy for a day to prepare his things and to bid his friends farewell.

The next day, having loaded his painting sup-plies onto the horse Lord Ganuan had offered him, Sakumat mounted his own old, black horse, which had been spending the later years of its life grazing peacefully at the edge of town.

The little caravan left behind the dale of Malatya, having crossed its flatland to the north, and began to climb the side of the broad northern valley. When the city had disappeared from sight behind them, they crossed a barren, parched region. A few stunted trees, like dying guardians of a conquered forest, stood out in the dull basin, which was cov-ered with long tracts of rose-grey gravel. Brown lizards darted over the rocks as the horses neared. Occasionally, the swiftly moving shadow of a falcon frightened off the few wild goats.

After a whole day of travelling, just after sunset, Sakumat and his guide reached the edge of a vast plateau, a sort of suspended valley surrounded by grim, grey peaks. However, the scenery suddenly changed. The land stretching out before them was less arid than below, with patches of pastures and even small vineyards.

In the centre, nestled away in the distance, a vil-lage of white stone enjoyed the refreshing coolness

of a cedar grove that rose up behind it like a gift from God. Between village and grove, even whiter than the other buildings, stood a huge palace, one as large as the greatest palace in Malatya, perhaps even larger.

Having crossed the farmlands and village streets, Sakumat was ushered into the palace. He admired the rich silence that reigned within, the cedar doors with gold decorations and the servants' pearly velvet jackets.

Then he was led into a cool, spacious room with a large window that looked out over the palace wall, beyond the village. It offered, at a single glance, a view of the entire plateau, all the way back to the mountains encircling it.

The lord of Nactumal was announced. In walked a tall man who looked the same age as the painter but had short, greying hair. A dark, bushy moustache grew from his face like the crop from a past planting season.

"You are welcome in my land and my home," said the burban. "Thank you for giving in to my messenger's insistence and accepting my invitation. If I were a good host, as I should be, I would let you rest this evening and all night long, thinking only

of your wellbeing. I would let this conversation wait until tomorrow morning. But anxiousness stirs in my breast, and like a strong young horse, the question I must ask you refuses to be still. I believe it will prance within my heart all night unless it is fed the hay that is your answer."

Sakumat smiled and bowed slightly. "Your hospitality is perfect, sire," he said. "As for your question, it will have an honest answer from me. And if it's simply impossible for me to give you one right away, then I'll have tonight to consider it, and so we'll have saved time. Now make your request, sire, because from all I've heard so far, it seems different from those I normally receive, and this has made me quite curious."

The burban also smiled, and he sat down on the room's carpet, which was as big as one to be found in a mosque. Sakumat sat down facing him.

"I have only one child, a young son named Madurer," the burban said slowly. "He suffers from a strange illness: every trace of sunshine and dust is harmful to him: his eyes swell, he grows short of breath, a rash and even sores form on his skin. He cannot go outdoors, and run and play in the palace gardens as my servants' children do.

Furthermore, he cannot live in a room like this, with a window that lets the mountain air and sunlight enter freely and abundantly. All the doctors in Turkey who boast science and knowledge have visited this palace. All have explained to me, each with great skill, the mysterious, incurable nature of his illness. Some have heard of similar cases in other lands or other times. Some speak of harmful substances that my son's body absorbs from the air, which the sunlight makes even more harmful. Yet what these substances are and how my child can be protected from them, they cannot say. They all strongly recommended that Madurer live in the most sheltered, innermost area of the palace. He can only breathe air filtered through layers of damp gauze, and he can have neither windows nor direct sunlight, only illumination from covered skylights. And so it has been. For over five years now, since his affliction first appeared, my son has never left this palace, nor has he ever been allowed to stand at a window and enjoy the sunlight or a view of the valley. No plants or flowers or even vine clippings are permitted in his quarters as decoration, since soil, pollen and leaves are harmful to him."

Having said this while looking Sakumat in the eye, the burban hung his head and fell silent for a long moment. The painter also sat in silence, waiting.

Ganuan looked up and said, "I would like my son's rooms to be decorated with pictures and colours. I heard passing merchants and hunters speak of your work. This is why I summoned you. You will have no cause to complain about my hospitality or your reward when you leave. I beg you to accept." Again the burban looked into Sakumat's eyes and sighed deeply. His right hand, strong and dark, gripped his studded leather belt as one would grip the reins of a rebellious horse.

"May I ask a question, sire?" said the painter.

"All my attention is yours, and I will answer with all the truth within me," the burban said.

"What do you wish me to paint in your son's rooms?"

"Of that I have given no thought," the burban said. "Your art and imagination may decide."

"Here is another question. What is your son's spirit like? Does his situation, so difficult for a child, make him unhappy? And are his face and body, as one might imagine, stunted and frail, like plants given no sunlight?"

For a moment the burban half closed his eyes. His grip on his belt relaxed. "These questions I will not answer, my friend," he said, "not because I do not wish to, but because a father's words are never those that best describe his child. Upon hearing them, you would be bound to wonder how great is my illusion and how deceitful my affection. But given that, unless I am mistaken, you have generously granted my wish, you will have your answer directly from the body and face and spirit of my beloved son. In the morning you will see for yourself."

Madurer was a pale boy but not an unhappy one. He was almost eleven, yet his life of seclusion had slowed the growth of his body, and his features were those of a nine-year-old child. There was nothing stunted or frail about him though: his face was bright and graceful, his eyes steady and dark, his hair thick and raven-black. His complexion was as fair as his father's. The linen robes he wore were embroidered with threads of a hundred colours, the result of the excellent craftsmanship of the elderly

women who looked after him and kept the rooms in which he lived spotlessly clean.

When the burban took Sakumat to see him, the boy kissed his father's hands and greeted the stranger with a little bow, looking at him with curiosity.

"Madurer," the burban said, holding one of his son's hands in his own, "I promised you a gift for your eleventh birthday and told you it would be a surprise, so that your anticipation would make you enjoy it all the more. It is almost your birthday. The man beside me is Sakumat, a painter of great skill who lives in Malatya, to the south. I summoned him and asked that he decorate your rooms with his artistry. He has brought many brushes and paints with him, and his hands are like a magician's. Last night he accepted my request. And so, you will have the joy of watching him paint, and the pictures he creates will be a beautiful backdrop for your rooms."

Madurer looked at Sakumat again, this time a bit longer. Then he kissed his father's hand again and said, "Father, I want to tell you two things. But as you listen to the first, remember there will be a second. The first is this: in the last few days, when

imagining the gift you promised me, I thought—
who knows why, or maybe because I wished it
so—that you were going to bring me a musician
who played the *kubikal*, the kind you hear from
afar, in the streets of the village. Maybe I thought
so because when you were telling me about the
surprise, your eyes were looking up at the walls but
seemed to be seeing something else. I thought you
were thinking of the village and the musician who
could be heard playing just then. Instead you were
thinking of paintings. Father, I was so convinced I'd
guessed your plans that I was already daydreaming
of how I would sit before the musician, listening to
his music, and how I would astonish him by asking
him to play again and again, without ever tiring of
it, like little children do. So now I should be sad,
because that isn't your gift.

"But the second thing, Father, is that I'm not
the least bit sad, because I've never even imagined
paintings in my rooms. It's a gift I never would have
dreamed of and in comparison, the *kubikal* player
seems no better than a wooden doll to me. And so
I thank you, Father, and I thank the man beside
you. What you both bring me is so beautiful and
new that my feet won't stay still!"

This said, little Madurer quickly kissed his father's hand a third time, and before the two men could say anything he broke into an excited dash along the walls, racing in and out of the room, laughing and spinning around like a puppy overcome with joy.

Ganuan brushed his lips against his hand where the boy had kissed it, and he smiled. "Here is the answer to your questions, my friend," he said. "I thank the Creator for this child. I would not want a different one, not even one with wings like the angels on Mount Ararat. Now you see why I had to insist, and how beautiful is this joy. But now I will take my leave, giving the two of you time to become friends. From now on, Sakumat, ask for anything it is within a man's power to give and it will be yours."

Once the burban was gone, Sakumat stood there waiting as Madurer continued his happy jaunt. It was as if the boy wished to express his happiness and shout it out from every corner of his rooms. Sakumat watched him, surprised and amused, like a horse trainer admiring a powerful colt bucking inside a corral. When the boy occasionally disappeared from his sight, the painter glanced at the blank walls of the room around him and tried to

imagine shapes and colours, but the large surfaces remained blank even in his mind, as though their whiteness was more powerful than his imagination and was dissolving his ideas.

Slightly troubled, Sakumat noticed that the boy's merry shouting had stopped. He expected to see him burst in through the broad, arched doorway to the next room, but all was quiet, and the whiteness of the walls seemed like the colour of that silence.

He craned his neck around the doorway but saw no one. Then he glimpsed a tuft of dark hair disappearing behind a projection in the wall. Darting back, he flattened himself against the wall and waited. From a few yards away came a faint panting. He didn't move. The tuft of hair cautiously reappeared, followed by Madurer's enthusiastic face beneath it.

"Boo!" the painter cried, leaping forward.

The boy shrieked with surprise, then burst out laughing and ran back through the doorway leading from the second room into the third. Sakumat also crossed through it, without rushing, and entered the last room, whose walls were as immaculate as those of the first two.

Madurer was hiding behind a curved projection in the wall to the right, just below one of the long slits through which, higher above, the white daylight seeped in, filtered through layers of gauze.

"I know where you are..." Sakumat said, but he intentionally turned his back on the hiding place and walked away from it. From behind him, he heard the boy's excited breathing, his playful squeal. "I'm going to find you, Madurer... You're definitely hiding behind this vase," said Sakumat, tiptoeing up to a large, enamelled urn half-filled with water, keeping his back to the boy's real hiding place.

He heard Madurer's breathless, victorious dash as the boy crossed the room and went back to hide in the second one.

"Oh, you aren't here, you sneaky salamander!" the painter exclaimed, pretending to be disappointed. He gave the boy a little time to find a new place to hide and then followed after him.

In the following days, Sakumat and Madurer spent lots of time together, playing and talking.

"What are you going to paint, Sakumat?" the boy asked.

"I don't know yet, Madurer. I've thought about it a great deal, but my mind is still blank, as white as the walls of this room."

"But you are going to paint something, aren't you?"

"Of course, Madurer. But first we need to talk about it, you and I. We need to decide what it is we want."

They played many games together, walked around the three rooms, sat at the low table which, apart from Madurer's bed and a low, long bookcase, was the only piece of furniture.

Madurer was an excellent chess player. From their first game, Sakumat saw that the boy was far better than he was. Each move that cost the man silent reflection was met with a quick, effective, almost amused response from the young boy.

As the two were engrossed in their games, silently slipping through the rooms were the elderly women, who changed the linens and curtains, and cleaned every corner. The gauze that filtered the air and light was replaced every day.

"What do you wish to see around you?" Sakumat asked. "What do your eyes long for?"

"Lots of things, and they're a bit confused... I've looked at all sorts of pictures in the books my father, the burban, has given me. I own almost a hundred books, and many of them are in colour, and there isn't a single picture I haven't looked at carefully over a dozen times. I've seen enchanting

images of the world: the sea, the mountains, big green fields and shimmering lakes. I know the shapes of the trees in our land and those in distant lands too. I've seen pictures of men in strange clothing, people in places far, far away, plus all kinds of animals. All these pictures seem like beautiful things I could wish for, Sakumat, and they're all crowded together in my mind. I can't choose..."

There was a pause.

"Maybe there's no need to choose, my young friend," the painter said. "All you need to do is put the pictures, and your wishes, in order."

"What do you mean, Sakumat?"

The painter fell silent again, stroking his face with his hand. Since arriving in the land of Nactumal, he'd let his beard grow, and grey-flecked stubble now covered his cheeks.

"This room has big walls, Madurer," he said. "If you want, I can paint the sea, the mountains and the lakes. I can paint many of the pictures you're familiar with. But first you need to tell me about the things you've seen, the pictures that are dear to you. You need to take me on a journey through your mind. Then we'll decide, and I'll help you."

That day, Madurer began to tell stories. He suggested to the painter that they look at the illustrations in his books together, but Sakumat preferred that he put them into words. And so, Madurer spoke about mountains and valleys, hillsides covered with orchards, dense forests and tilled fields, villages with white rooftops and red rooftops, and lively streets lined with tall trees bending in the wind.

Without realizing it, he was combining the images from his books with others he'd never seen but only imagined, landscapes from the tales told to him by the servants or his father, places that were wild and wonderful, immense and strange.

"I love the image of the sea," he said one day. "When I think of it, so vast, all blue and green, it's like joy enters my mind and fills it up."

Sakumat listened, asked questions, wanted details.

"Now I have a fairly good idea of what I'm going to paint, Madurer," he said after some time, "but I think we need to make a decision."

"A decision? About what?"

"My friend, we have in mind the mountains, the sea... These things are certainly too big, but

then again we shouldn't settle for tiny pictures. If we were to paint everything on a single wall, we would end up with a ridiculously small sea and puny mountains. We would have to squint—I as I paint them, and you as you look at them. And so, I propose painting each of the walls in this room, so we have more space and can feast our eyes on larger pictures."

"Of course!" cried Madurer. "In fact, why don't—"

He fell into confused silence.

"Don't hold back your words," Sakumat encouraged him.

"But I'm afraid what I'd like would be too much of a burden for you."

"Speak freely, Madurer. Listening to words isn't a burden. As for the rest, we'll see."

"Well, I just thought... if what you say is true, why don't we paint every part of the walls in all my rooms? Like the sky is everywhere, understand? That way the pictures could be even bigger, and filled with lots of things."

Sakumat reflected, stroking his beard. "That's a good idea, Madurer. As for the time it will take, we aren't in a hurry, are we?"

The boy smiled and didn't add a word.

"Well, now we really need to put our plans in order," Sakumat said.

"Explain that to me, Sakumat. I don't understand what kind of order you mean."

"Madurer," the painter said, "we want to paint the world. And so, just like the world, the painting needs to flow from one picture to the next naturally, without jumbling them together like pages torn from a book and scattered by the wind. This way, the gaze will be like a traveller moving calmly from one land to the next, without skipping around or having bothersome gaps."

Madurer was silent for a long time, thinking. Then he said, "Sometimes, Sakumat, I have dreams. In my dreams, the pictures jumble together strangely, and they get confused, and they change over and over."

After a pause, Sakumat asked, "Do you want us to paint the pictures like they are in dreams, Madurer?"

The boy hesitated. Then he smiled and said, "No. Let's paint the world. I'll do the dreaming myself."

And so they explored the walls of the rooms as if they were the open space of the skies. They began to imagine and arrange the subjects to be painted.

"Here we'll put the pasture full of sweet-smell-ing flowers."

"Yes, Sakumat! Like the one in the story about Mutkul the shepherd!"

"Then we'll paint Mutkul the shepherd's hut too. Teeny tiny, with his herd of red goats... Mutkul's goats were red, weren't they?"

"Yes. And will we paint his lame dog too, Sakumat?"

"Of course."

"It's going to be wonderful! But... from so far away, how will we be able to tell he's lame?"

"We might not be able to see that, Madurer, but we'll see the dog and we'll know it's Mutkul the shepherd's lame dog."

"Then over on this side, will we have the mountains?"

"Yes. And at the foot of the mountains, a village. Should we make it big or small?"

"Not too small, but not too big either, Sakumat. Not too big, because otherwise it'll take up all our space."

"We have space. We'll make it just the right size. We'll put in the minaret too."

"With the muezzin atop it, singing?"

29

"Naturally. What's a minaret without the muezzin atop it? A teeny tiny muezzin with a long nose."

"And we'll know he has a long nose, even if he's teeny tiny!"

"Behind the village, before the rocks, there should be a forest full of foxes and bears."

"Yes! But Sakumat..."

"What's wrong, my young friend?"

"I just thought of something. A minute ago, you said that, like the world, a painting shouldn't skip around."

"That's right, unless we want to paint the images of dreams."

"No, let's paint the world. But look, Sakumat: the wall ends here in the corner and takes a sharp turn in the other direction!"

"Yes, I see that, Madurer," the painter said, smiling.

"But the pictures are bound to have a gap here! It'll be like the meadow and the mountains suddenly change direction in the sky and disappear, or like the sea suddenly plunges down over the edge, understand?"

"I understand, Madurer, but I don't think there's anything we can do about it."

"Why do you say that? These corners will be a real bother for us! I'll ask my father, the burban, to have the corners of the walls rounded off! That way they'll be smooth, and the mountains can curve gently, like a traveller as he walks along, and the view won't suddenly be lost in empty space. And the sea won't plunge down. Wouldn't that be better, Sakumat?"

"Yes, it would be better, I think. But do you really believe the burban will agree to have all the corners of the walls removed, Madurer?"

"Of course he will. We have a good reason."

All the corners were rounded off. The walls now stretched out around Madurer and Sakumat, providing a smooth, flowing space.

As the servants attended to this work, the burban called for the painter and said this: "I summoned you to my home to give my son an unusual gift. Now I see it is becoming a miraculous gift. I confess that after a number of days, seeing nothing appear on the walls, my fatherly impatience made me think, *Despite his fame, this man is nothing but an*

*idler, taking advantage of my hospitality and cruelly toying with my dear son's spirit*. For these thoughts, I beg your forgiveness, but the fear that Madurer might suffer made them seep into my mind, just as a wound oozes with blood and black bile."

"What makes you say now, burban, that the gift to your son is miraculous?" Sakumat asked calmly. "Still today, if you were to search for brushstrokes on the walls of his rooms, you wouldn't find a single one. And as you were so honest in sharing your thoughts with me, I'll confess to you that in the beginning, for many days, my mind remained blank and useless, as though I had never held a brush in my hand or admired and copied the shape of a flower. Then, one night, troubled by that emptiness, I decided to give up and leave your home the next morning at dawn. That happened before the beginning of this moon."

"Yes," Ganuan said, nodding, "I know now that your mind and my son's are full of marvellous images and figures. I know that if you were to paint even a tenth of what you have imagined together, yours will be an admirable work indeed."

He said this with a small burst of joy. Then he paused, smiling, and added, "Often, in silence,

I go into Madurer's rooms. From a distance I listen as the two of you talk, and I watch as you make broad gestures at the blank walls, describing the pictures that will come to life there. I never go too close, but I believe that at these moments even if I were to go but one step behind you, you would have no idea I was there. Absorbed with you in this joyful work of imagination, my son might not even notice his father's presence. Do not think that this saddens me. In fact, it brings me great joy, because I have never seen Madurer as lively and cheerful as he has been while making these plans with you. He has always been a boy with a rich, lively imagination, but now he seems to be enjoying a sort of wonderful echo: in some mysterious way, the joy coming from within seems to flow back over him, making him happy. This is how, unseen though not hidden, I watch and learn your game, admiring your excellent planning and your wise curiosity."

Ganuan fell silent, pouring a cup of cool tea for his guest. They drank, looking each other in the eye, as the men of that land did, to silently express their respect and esteem, and to show they neither felt fear nor intended to cause it.

"But now, my friend," the burban said seriously, putting down the precious teacup, "it is plain to see that your game has grown, and that it may call for more time and effort than you or I could have expected. I wish you to continue, but I think with concern, *Perhaps Sakumat has other work to do in his city, or promises to keep there. Perhaps he has people who love him and await his return, people his heart longs to see again.* This is what I think, and it is a torment. You know, my friend, how much I appreciate what you are doing, all the more because it goes well beyond the gift I intended to give. But if one or all of the things I have imagined are so important to you that they make you rush your work or abandon it before it is finished, with sadness in my heart I beg you not to begin it at all and to leave my house at once. This would allow me to find a good excuse and the right moment to disappoint my son, at a time when, as happens with children, the disappointment will last no more than a few days. Even if you do so, naturally you will be paid what you would have received for working in my house for a year.

"But if it is at all possible for you to continue the work you have begun, and to give it all the time it

needs, I beg you with love and humility to stay. If you have a family, or people dear to you, I will have them brought here and will welcome them into my home as my brother's family, and for as long as necessary. Or if you prefer, I will have a cool, comfortable villa by the woods placed at their disposal and yours. I will put five men at your service, and three women to tend to the food and housework. You will be given all the horses your heart desires, and they will be yours forever. Once it is finished, whenever that may be, the payment I give you will make you a wealthy man."

Sakumat didn't reply right away. His beard now covered his cheeks and chin and what, during its first days, had been a rough gesture had now become a calm, customary caress made while or before he spoke.

"I too, burban, see that the game has grown larger," the painter said, "and I know that to complete it I'll need to be like a silent genie, even more obliging than the one that came out of Aladdin's lamp. But I too have been swept up in the game, my lord. I stand at its edge like a thirsty man stands before a cool, gushing fountain. I have neither wife nor family in Malatya, and my friends

will think of me while I'm gone, and will know I'm thinking of them too. As for the riches you promise, I can tell you that a painter has but one mouth to enjoy the flavours of food and but one belly to comfort. Those who spend time admiring the land and the trees and the changing sky in all its splendour feel no need of any other form of abundance. Instead, sire, there is something I would ask."

"You have my ear," the burban said, bowing slightly.

"I've found that staying in the magnificent room you've put at my disposal does nothing for me. In fact, I spend little time there because I pass my days visiting and talking with your son. What's more, the view I enjoy from that room, though wonderful, in some way distracts and impoverishes my mind, which is dedicated to creating a view of the world with Madurer. And so, if you have no objections, I would ask that a carpet be laid out for me in your son's rooms so I may pass every moment of my time with him, as is fitting for a close friendship. That way I won't miss the chance to chat with him in the mornings, and hear him remember his dreams, which so quickly fade,

or to chat with him in the evenings, when peace and wisdom unite."

The burban smiled and bowed his head three times as a sign of his heartfelt approval.

This was the agreement between Ganuan, lord of Nactumal, and Sakumat the painter. Meanwhile, young Madurer, in his still-spotless rooms, stared at the walls from where he lay on the cushions. He gazed at them eagerly and with breathless delight, as a boy might look into the eyes of the girl he loves.

Madurer's rooms, which were sealed off and protected, as we know, were three in number and all the same shape and size. Coming in through the long, tall skylights shielded by pure-white gauze was an abundance of uniform light that filled the space with a milky glow. The only way in from the rest of the palace was an arched entrance in the first room, reached by crossing through three curtains positioned a step apart from each other, a triple

obstacle for the air from the outside. Between one room and the other there were no curtains, but broad, square doorways. Just as he had done with the corners of the rooms, the burban had had their edges rounded off.

Altogether, the three rooms were so large that if Madurer walked all the way around them he could count almost a hundred paces.

The boy's bed was in the centre of the first room. A few steps from Madurer's bed was the low bookcase in ivory, full of books and toys. It was there, beside the bookcase, that Sakumat had them place his carpet. During the day, the two friends would cover it with silk cushions and sit there to stare at the walls and play games.

It was also to this room, the first one, that three times a day Ganuan would come to talk and play with his son. And twice a day the father and son would eat together, along with Sakumat, at a low table which the servants would carry into the second room, the meal already laid out upon it.

"Where do we begin, Madurer?" the painter asked one morning, after many days of planning and conversation.

"Are we really ready, Sakumat?" the boy asked.

"See all these paintbrushes? And we have so many kinds of paint. Your father, the burban, has given us the most precious coloured oils and pigments which the merchants bring from Persia on their camels."

"That's not what I meant, Sakumat. I'm asking if... if we're sure what to paint."

"We have some ideas, Madurer."

"Yes, of course. But we can't do it wrong."

"Why do you say that? Why can't we do it wrong?"

"Because if we do it wrong... if we don't make the pictures like they should be made, we'll be stuck with them forever."

Sakumat raised one hand. He said, "But we *can* do it wrong, Madurer. We just need to keep our eyes open and notice our mistakes. Shapes conceal shapes, paint covers paint. But now we need to begin. Unless we begin, we can't do things right—or even wrong, for that matter."

"Yes," the boy said. "That's true."

"So, where do we begin? Which wall should we paint first?"

"This one! No, that one! Or maybe... You see,

Sakumat? I'm already getting it wrong and we haven't even started yet!"

"You're not getting it wrong, Madurer. You're deciding. That's always difficult, but you can do it."

Sakumat waited in silence. The boy had grown very serious.

"Let's start with this wall," he finally said. "Here, to the right of the door."

"Fine. And what should we paint?"

There was more silence.

Madurer licked his lips and breathed deeply, his eyes opened wide.

Sakumat's hands were resting on a cushion in front of him. "We spoke of many places, remember?" he said.

"Yes, I remember. But wait a moment, please. It's very hard to choose."

"We aren't in a hurry, Madurer. No hurry at all."

"Let's start with the mountain. Remember when we talked about the flowery field and Mutkul the shepherd? Let's make the mountain where Mutkul lives!"

"Only that, Madurer?"

"No, of course not! The mountains around it too. Not all the mountains in the world... Let's just make *some* mountains."

Sakumat asked no further questions. He went to work. Using a piece of charcoal he drew the lines of a large valley, sketching rocky peaks around it. With delicate strokes he outlined wooded areas and added tilled fields at the bottom of the valley. He drew a cluster of stone houses and a road that wound its way up the mountain, concealed from time to time by rocky bends.

Behind him, Madurer watched with fascination. Now and then he shifted restlessly, his head and body following the charcoal lines on the wall. Then, finally calm, he sat down on the cushions and watched, his eyes narrowed, enjoying Sakumat's swift additions, admiring the creation and expansion of the places in the picture.

"What's that, Sakumat?"

"It's a boulder, perhaps. Or a hut. Would you like it to be a hut?"

"Could it really be a hut?"

"Of course. It's near a big field. It could be the farmer's hut."

"But Sakumat, is it really a hut? Did you mean to make it a hut? It looks like a boulder."

"It's only a sketch, Madurer. Nothing's finished yet. It could be a boulder, and it could be the farmer's hut." The painter, with light strokes, added contours and turned it into a hut.

"It's the hut of one of Mutkul's friends!" Madurer burst out excitedly.

"What's his name?" Sakumat asked without turning around. "I don't remember Mutkul having any friends."

"True, there weren't any in the story! But Mutkul could've had a farmer friend, right?"

"Of course he could. He was a sociable man, even if he was happy enough with just his goats and his dog."

"Then let's make believe he's called Insubat!"

"Yes, this is Insubat's hut. Did Insubat have a large herd?"

"No, because he wasn't a shepherd, he was a farmer. He had an ox to pull his plough, and an old donkey with a furry snout."

Sakumat sketched quickly. "There! This is the little pen for the ox and the donkey," he said. "It's here, behind the hut."

Madurer was on his feet again, looking eagerly at the wall. "So where do we put Mutkul's hut?"

"We'll think about that later today, Madurer," the painter said. "Right now, we're a little tired. Besides, the burban will be here soon."

In the afternoon, as they were looking through a book with lots of pictures of long-legged insects, the boy asked, "What about the big boulder, Sakumat?"

"What boulder?"

"The one that... the one that could've been a boulder but became Insubat's hut instead. The one that wasn't the hut yet... I mean, the boulder that could've been..."

"Yes, I remember. What do you want to know?"

"Where is it?"

"I don't know, Madurer. It didn't exist yet. Something was there, and we decided it was Insubat's hut. There's only Insubat's hut now."

"But the boulder could've been there too, right? And if it isn't there, where is it? I mean, it doesn't exist at all? It just... isn't?"

Sakumat was about to reply, but held back. He was quiet for a moment. Then he said, "Maybe it's on the other end of the mountain. It's on the side we can't see."

47

Madurer went back to leafing through his book. "Let's say it's on the other side of the mountain, then," he said, "the side where there are cattle thieves too. It's right there, in a cedar grove. It's never completely covered by sunlight because the cedar branches grow really close together."

"It must be quite mossy then," Sakumat said.

"What colour is moss?" the boy asked, still looking through the book. "I've read that it's green, but is it green like this butterfly? Is moss this shade of green?"

"A bit darker. It looks like the green in... this part of the picture. But there are many kinds of moss, and a lighter shade of moss is bound to exist. Maybe there's moss the same shade as that butterfly."

"Have you seen any?"

"No. There isn't much moss around here. But farther south and even to the north, high up in the mountains, there's lots of it. That's what travellers say."

Madurer looked up. "If it really does exist," he said, "and this butterfly lands on it, nobody can see him because they're the same colour."

"Yes, that's right," said Sakumat. "Like a lizard on a rock."

Madurer giggled. Then he asked, "Do you think the butterfly knows he exists when he's on the light green moss?"

Sakumat laughed too. "Yes, I think he knows he exists as much as he does when he's flying or he lands beside a droplet of water."

"Well, I think he knows it a little less," Madurer said, still giggling softly.

Days passed, and mountains were born. Not only the valley where Insubat and Mutkul lived, and the slopes on which the lame dog raced, barking after the herd, but many other valleys and peaks, huts and fences, goats that could be seen, snakes that couldn't be seen, cliffsides and ponds with salamanders. It all slowly came to life, made of what Madurer and Sakumat knew of and imagined and wished for, sketching, changing, drawing, painting.

The movement of Sakumat's hand was calm. It knew how to wait for the pictures—through words, laughter and memories—to be decided together.

The whiteness of the first wall disappeared, and in its place rose a mountainous part of the world, a space well balanced between the close and the infinite, between the deep and the towering.

Each brushstroke had created a dimension, a direction and a truth.

The picture didn't stop. Gliding across the curve that connected the walls, the mountains continued, changing in texture and tone, dipping into dusky hillsides barren of woods and full of stones. Flatlands then stretched out, with sparse shacks and distant, white-walled villages, much like those of Nactumal.

In the foreground—actually, in the background, because in the foreground there was a radiant sensation of air, a transparence worthy of notice—a nomad cart with a blue curtain crossed a little wooden bridge that spanned a river. It was an illustration Madurer had found in one of his books. The boy loved it so much and looked at it so often that Sakumat had copied it onto the wall. But to the little pepper-coloured horse trotting along, tethered to

the back of the cart, he'd added a girl with a red kerchief on her head. Her name was Talya.

"Where's the cart going, Madurer?"

"It's going far, far away, Sakumat."

"Yes, but is it heading toward the hills over there, or in the other direction?"

"Why do you ask?"

"You see, here, around the bend, the road hasn't been drawn yet. We can have it keep going toward the hills, like this, making a wide turn and heading up to that village, or we can make it go to the right, toward the new wall."

"What will be on the new wall, Sakumat?"

"The world will continue. We thought of putting a plain there, didn't we? Land and more land, as far as the eye can see."

"Yes. Make the road lead toward the plain," the boy said. "That's where Talya's cart is going. Once it's down there, Talya will get off her little horse and pick flowers. But please, make a road that leads toward the village too. The cart will take the other one, but because it wants to, not because there's only one road."

"Of course, Madurer. There isn't only one road in the world."

The third wall, and also the fourth, became a plain. It took up two walls because it was a very large plain and contained so many things: two villages, one near and one far away; fields of grain and tobacco; windmills like the ones in distant Holland. It was toward the windmills that Talya's cart was heading as it travelled a road that crossed fields and villages, skirting a green river until, on the fourth wall, to the left of the entrance beside which the painting had started, it reached a city under siege.

Soldiers and their brightly coloured camps surrounded the yellowish walls of the fortified city, batteries of stout cannons fired cannonballs, and bands of horsemen raised a whirlwind of dust around it all. There was even a catapult, and a wooden tower from which archers were shooting arrows at the city's defenders. Yet the besieged were defending themselves well, and it was clear they would manage to hold out for a long time to come.

Atop the city walls, unconcerned by the arrows and cannon fire, beautiful, elegant women looked down, staring at the enemy camp as though watching a town parade. And, upon closer inspection,

what were the besieger cavalrymen doing if not manoeuvres that might earn the admiration of the tiny ladies above? What other point was there in prancing around outside the impenetrable city? Did they perhaps think they could leap up and bring the attack inside? The walls were so tall and well-fortified that the poor infantrymen, farther off, were falling in clusters in their attempt to scale them, ending up splashing around like geese in the moat.

Sakumat spent three months painting the siege. It was a very complicated scene and every day he added characters, events, stories to tell.

Then, with the addition of a tiny besieger prince sending a message by carrier pigeon to a besieged princess, that part of the work was finished.

Would the pigeon succeed in flying unharmed through the turbulent skies of battle? Many arrows, from above and below, were heading in its direction. Many projectiles were whizzing along their fated courses, regardless of its white feathers.

Sakumat and Madurer knew that soldiers often grew weary when making war, that they would rather aim at a bird, which would fall without a cry, than at the many suits of armour of their enemies,

with the risk of striking them and hearing their screams and seeing their blood pour out as though from a cracked ewer.

However, for the time being the pigeon was there, snowy and pure in its first yards of flight. And leaning out from an embrasure, leaning out from hope, the princess watched it approach and protected it with her gaze.

By now eight months had passed since Sakumat's arrival in Nactumal, but the picture, wrapping around the curved edge of the doorway, didn't stop. Like an open horizon, the plain swept through it and into the second room, moving away from windmills and sieges, and rising in the form of gently rolling hills.

"Why more hills, Sakumat?" the boy said. "Didn't we decide the sea would begin in this room?"

Sakumat didn't reply, swiftly continuing the drawing. But before long, the gentle line of the hills cut off in a clear break, plunging downward in an almost sheer cliff. Then, holding the charcoal loosely between his fingers, the painter drew a thin, continuous, perfectly horizontal line across the entire wall.

"Here's the sea, Madurer."

The boy watched as the horizon was born. "Please, don't stop," he said.

Sakumat had already passed the curve between the walls. "Farther?" he asked without turning around.

"Yes, farther! Across that whole wall, and the next one too... please!" Madurer said. "Let's make the whole sea in this room."

Sakumat didn't stop. Slowly, steadily, he drew the horizontal line all the way around, breaking off at the entrance to the third room and continuing on the other side, until he was back at the doorway between the second room and the first. "There. The whole sea," he said.

Madurer, standing in the centre of the room, slowly turned all the way around, staring intently at the faint line that divided the white space of the walls. He turned around several times, his face flushed, his eyes shining, his hands grasping at the air fitfully. "Above is the sky, and below is the sea," he said.

Suddenly, with one of his swift, graceful movements, he dashed into the first room and tugged on a cord suspended near the main entrance. An instant later, the eldest of his female servants stepped inside.

"Alika! Bring my father, quickly!" said the boy.

"Are you unwell, my young lord?" the woman asked, studying his face.

"I'm very well, Alika," Madurer said. "I just want my father to come so I can show him something. Hurry, please!"

**8**

"Are the fish infinite, Sakumat?"

"Infinite? No," the painter replied, adding dabs of blue-green to the sea, "but certainly no one could count them all."

"Something that can't be counted *is* infinite!" Madurer exclaimed.

The sea was now completed. All the way around the room, down to the floor, a strip of intense blue, rippled at points, shimmered beneath the different blue of the sky. Billowing clouds covered part of it,

drifting in from afar, spreading over the horizon like a radiant blossom. Gazing across the sea, one saw different colours. Navy in some areas, in others clear aqua, then a pale greenish blue edged with wisps of froth.

"Should we add some fish, Madurer?"

"That's impossible, Sakumat. The fish are down in the water, and we can't see them."

"But we're in the water too, in a way. We're partly above it and partly in it."

"No, it's like we're in a glass boat," the boy said. "We're floating right on the surface of the sea."

"Sometimes fish jump out," the painter replied. "Even whales take giant leaps, and dolphins and swordfishes dart out of the water in schools, like a rainbow. They follow alongside ships, even glass boats. Then there's the flying fish, which can soar hundreds of yards through the air before diving back down into the sea..."

"Do you like painting fish, Sakumat?" Madurer asked, looking at him.

The painter smiled. "Yes, very much. You could tell?"

"But I think... maybe it's better for the fish to stay in the sea. Because... well, I can't explain why."

"Perhaps, Madurer, you think that if we painted the fish they wouldn't move, but down below they're swimming around swiftly, and they're infinite."

Madurer was the one smiling now. "Maybe that's why, Sakumat," he said.

And so nothing interrupted the line of the sea, which crowned almost the entire second room like it went on forever.

Winter was on its way and the air in the high valley grew chillier. At night they slept beneath soft fur skins, and Alika brought the child and the painter wonderfully soft woollen robes. The two friends used them not only to cover themselves but also as costumes when playing, and together they created amusing characters by filling the robes with silk cushions.

The sea was finished in November, eleven months after the painter had begun his work.

"What's that?" Madurer asked one morning, after staring silently for a long time at a particular stretch of the horizon.

"That? It's the sea."

"No, that!" the boy said, pointing. "That tiny dot on the horizon, just to the left of the cloud.

Do you see it?" He ran over and tapped on it. Then he returned to the cushions, beside his friend.

Outside the palace, clouds swept across the sky over the valley, even if no wind could be heard, and they covered and uncovered the sun. Though it was filtered and indirect, the light in the room dimmed and then grew full again, making the sea swell.

"I don't know what that is, Madurer," the painter said. "I hadn't seen it before. It must be something, though. Isn't it a bird?"

"No. If it was a bird, it would be a little above the horizon, or completely invisible. You can't see birds so far in the distance. What could it be, Sakumat? Could it be an island far, far away?"

"Of course. Or an island that isn't too far away but is tiny."

"Or it could be a ship!"

"Yes."

"How can we tell, Sakumat?"

"We simply wait. If it's still right there tomorrow, that means it's an island. If it's gone, or it's moved closer, it's a ship."

"Let's wait, then."

The next morning, as soon as he woke up, the boy ran over to the wall. "It's still there! Look! It's gotten bigger. It's a ship sailing toward us!"

"At least for now," Sakumat said. "It might change course, grow small again, and disappear."

Without saying a word, Madurer walked over and hit him with a silk cushion. He laughed and hit him again and again as Sakumat ducked his head to defend himself from the gentle blows. Then Madurer went back to the wall, where the dot on the sea was only slightly bigger than it had been the day before.

"What kind of ship is it?"

"I don't know, Madurer."

"Maybe it's a pirate ship!"

"Like the one in the book with the red cover?"

"Yes, that kind. A brig, with thirty pirates aboard." The boy slowly backed away from the wall, staring at it. "It comes from the coasts of Greece and it's called the *Tigrez*."

The next morning, still tiny, the pirate ship stood out against the horizon, tilted slightly, its many sails full of wind. It was too far away for the pirates to be seen but its tiny flag was black, and the white speck in the centre of it could only have been a skull.

"Sakumat, I think the pirates aboard the *Tigrez* are being too cautious," Madurer said.

"Why?"

"Because they only sail at night, and by day they just wait there in the sun the whole time, even though there's a strong wind blowing. They must be bored, don't you think? And they won't know what to do. The more rebellious ones will huddle in the shadows of the hatch and begin to plot a mutiny. 'What the devil is the captain doing?' they'll say. 'What the blasted devil of a way of sailing is this? Have cuttlefish crawled into his brain?'"

Sakumat smiled. "Yes," he said. "It truly is a strange way of sailing."

"I think we could encourage them a little. Want to?" the boy asked.

And so Sakumat painted the ship bigger as the boy watched, and in three days the *Tigrez* had moved a good deal closer, in a week by at least another mile, and each time, given that the wind was changing, its sails stretched out in a different direction and its keel cut through the waves at a different angle. For it to come very close—as close as possible for a cautious ship, that is—it took a whole month.

The book about pirates spread open on his lap, Madurer made suggestions and asked questions. Rarely did Sakumat reply with words.

There weren't thirty pirates aboard the *Tigrez*, actually, but twenty-nine. Only eighteen of them could be seen on deck, because the others were down below, in the galley or their berths, and some were even in irons, as punishment. Still, Madurer knew all their names and where each of them came from.

The captain was a Greek from Salamis and was named Krapulos. The first mate was a renegade from Rhodes by the name of Purtik. They were both on the little quarterdeck, peering out at sea through a big spyglass, while teetering up in the crow's nest, his arm stretched out toward the east, was Randui the Moor, whom the pirates had freed from a Turkish prison.

"No cabin boy aboard this ship?" Sakumat asked one day.

Madurer looked up from the book he was thumbing through. Now sailing upwind, the vessel had veered to the side and stood out in all its glory. Eight pirates worked the rigging, in great danger of tumbling into the sea.

"Should there be one?" the boy asked.

"Of course. All captains, when they were little, worked as a cabin boy aboard a pirate ship. No little cabin boys, no great captains."

"Was even Krapulos a cabin boy?"

"He was cabin boy aboard the *Majada*, a brig known as 'The Shark of Cyprus'," Sakumat explained. "When the Turkish ships of Kuranin the Mad sank the *Majada*, Krapulos, who was fourteen years old, swam a whole night, following the stars until he reached the island of Santorini..."

The next day, boldly sitting astride the bowsprit of the *Tigrez* was a dark-haired boy clutching the tip of the jib with one hand and, with his other, the horn of the dragon that acted as the pirate ship's figurehead. It was the *Tigrez*'s cabin boy, and his name was Madurer.

"I'm not the only one in the world with this name, am I?" the boy had said excitedly.

"Of course not. Who knows how many Madurers there are," Sakumat had agreed.

"Well then, one of them is the cabin boy aboard the *Tigrez*," the boy had concluded, a big silk cushion gripped between his knees. And he stared out at the sea beyond the prow.

One night, Madurer woke up wailing. Sakumat and Alika found him covered in sweat, writhing in his bed in a violent, agonized state of half-sleep.

In the morning he was resting peacefully but was very pale. A trace of perspiration glistened on the edge of his lips and forehead.

With Sakumat, Ganuan kept vigil at his son's bedside.

"This happens to him at long intervals," the burban said, staring at the sleeping boy's face.

"At times, months go by, but never more than ten. Afterwards, for a week or two he is feeble and sleeps a great deal. In the end he returns to being as lively as ever. The doctors believe the cause is a build-up of the substances harmful to him. Though here in his rooms he is protected, there is no preventing every last trace of them from entering. These bouts of fever, the doctors say, purify him."

"I wonder, sire," Sakumat said, his head bowed, "whether the paints and pigments I'm using are harmful. I handle them with great care, but perhaps not enough care, given his fragile condition."

"Have no fear of that, my friend," the burban replied. "There is nothing in this attack that has not been seen before, nor did it happen any sooner—in fact, this is the longest period between bouts we have ever witnessed. What's more, from the very start I looked into that possibility, and everyone said the paints posed no risk whatsoever. They are a source of nothing but joy for my son."

It was as the burban had predicted: over the following days, though Madurer stayed in bed, drained of energy, he showed no further signs of suffering. Between his periods of peaceful slumber,

which lasted almost half the day, he resumed his talks with the painter.

"Now we need to paint the third room, Sakumat."

"Yes. How shall we paint it?"

"I've been thinking about that a lot. I'm deciding."

"There's no hurry, my young friend. You're tired, and I'm a little tired too. No harm will be done if we postpone the work for a while."

"Yes, of course. But thinking isn't very tiring for me, so I'll think about it."

The boy asked that his bed be taken into the third room, whose walls were still untouched. He would stare at them for a long time, quietly, holding his hand to his mouth with a serious look on his face.

"May I know some of your thoughts, Madurer?" Sakumat asked after a while.

"Well, I... They aren't exactly thoughts, Sakumat. They're like wishes—wishes of pictures that are fighting each other, battling it out in my mind. I know one of them will win, but it's too soon to know which."

"Wouldn't you like to tell me about the pictures, Madurer? Perhaps words will make it easier to decide."

But the boy had dozed off again. His naps, so deep they could only have been caused by great exhaustion, never lasted less than two hours.

And so Sakumat would leave the palace and mount his old horse. He would slowly ride through the village, watched with perfectly silent curiosity by its inhabitants, who had some idea of why he was staying as a guest of the burban. When the painter nodded to the boldest of them—those who looked him in the eye—his greetings were met with hasty bows and bashful retreats.

Once out of the village, he would coax his horse into a brisker pace without ever urging it to a gallop. Aware of the creature's frailty, and his own weariness caused by the months he'd spent painting, he found it hard to feel the ease and enjoyment of riding he'd always had before. Still, he rode on, allowing his gaze to dart around far more swiftly than his horse, to silently strike the broad, rocky flanks of the valley, its image rebounding like a stark, steady, crystal-clear echo. And it felt like he was noticing stones and shades of colour with new precision, that somehow he could foresee the things the landscape was revealing to him little by little.

On his return, he would almost always find the boy still asleep and would stay at his bedside, waiting for him to awaken. If Madurer continued sleeping for a long while, Sakumat would spend the time walking along the painted walls of the rooms, his gaze going over every one of the pictures' rich details, every mark left there by the imaginative games played together with the boy.

"You know, Sakumat, at first I thought of painting the sea in the third room too," Madurer said, drawing a horizontal line in the air with his hand, "because the sea is really big and there's never enough of it. I thought we could put in a few islands and other ships. I liked the idea. We could've added dolphins and swordfishes, and even a whale leaping out. We could've made a sea like that, couldn't we?"

"Of course."

"But then, when I imagined the picture, I felt a little... dissatisfied, and I don't know why, but I thought even if there's never enough of the sea, all that sea would've been too much. The sea has... too much distance in it. It's too full of distance, understand?"

"I think so, Madurer. When looking at the sea, the eyes can't stay still, while the feet grow weary from too much stillness. I think I understand what you were feeling. And so?"

"And so, just like that, a different picture suddenly came to my mind: a picture of something like the sea, but with less distance. Something big, but near."

"And what's the picture, Madurer?"

"It's a meadow. With grass and flowers. Not like the ones we made on the mountains and hills, though. Those are seen from far away. I saw a meadow with grass and flowers very close up."

"A meadow that's big and close up," Sakumat repeated.

"Yes, like a sea, but near, understand? All the way around, so you can be in the middle of it. So you can be inside of it."

"We'll paint a meadow, then, Madurer."

74

"But there's something else. There's something I need to tell you... But I'm very tired right now. I'll tell you afterwards, Sakumat."

Sometimes during the wait, the painter wouldn't leave the palace. Completely free to move around as he pleased, he would walk down hallways and up stairways until he reached a tower that wasn't particularly tall, yet was far taller than any other building in the village, and there he would watch the birds in flight. He would watch them for so long, and with such attention, that upon returning to Madurer's rooms and finding the boy still asleep, he would take out large sheets of parchment and copy their flight patterns in sketches that no one else could have understood. Then he would fold the sheets and return them to the low bookcase in the first room.

Often, when Madurer awoke, as though he'd been inspired by curiosity in his sleep, the boy would ask that his bed be moved from one of the painted rooms to the other, or that it face a different direction, so he would have before him first the mountains and then the plain and the besieged city, or the deserted hillsides or the pirate ship with its shimmering sea or the pure marine horizon.

"What is it you wanted to tell me about the new meadow, Madurer?" Sakumat asked.

"It's going to be beautiful, isn't it? I think of it as beautiful."

"I think it's going to be very nice. You and I usually do nice things, don't we? But you had something else to tell me, remember?"

"Yes. It won't be very easy. I wouldn't want it to be too much trouble for you."

Sakumat smiled and waited without speaking.

The boy clasped his hands together on the covers, resting them gently on his belly. It was one of Sakumat's customary gestures, and Madurer often mimicked them, whether meaning to or not. "Remember the ship, when it arrived?" he asked.

"Of course I remember."

"I mean, remember how it came closer little by little? At first there was that speck in the distance, and we didn't even know it was a ship..."

"Yes, I remember it well."

"Then it got bigger, so you could see it was a ship."

"Yes. First it sailed only at night." Sakumat smiled. "Then we decided to encourage the crew."

The boy was knitting his brow, as though from effort. Sakumat quietly waited.

"I'd like it to be the same for the meadow," Madurer said all in one breath, spreading his fingers slightly on the covers.

Sakumat raised an eyebrow. "So if I thought you wanted a ship to sail in slowly through the meadow, would I be right or wrong?" he asked.

Madurer laughed. He sat up in bed and leaned back against the cushions. By now he'd grown quite strong again and his complexion, though not very colourful by nature, was no longer pale and sickly. "Wrong! I mean I really liked seeing the ship come closer, and I'd like to see the meadow grow little by little too."

"You'd like me to paint it slowly?"

"No... I'd really like it to be a meadow that grows. First with short grass, then taller grass. First with flowers that are—what can I call them?—unripe, and then in bloom. Understand?"

"Yes, now I understand," Sakumat said.

"Can we do it?"

"Yes. It will take time, though."

"Before the mountains, you said, *We have all the time we need, Madurer!*" the boy exclaimed, trying to imitate the painter's voice.

77

"That's true. We have time," Sakumat replied softly. "All the time that's granted us is ours."

"Would you summon the servants, please? I'd like to have my bed taken into the third room. I want to sleep there, while the meadow is growing. Will you sleep there too?"

"Hmm... At my age, a meadow might be too damp at night, Madurer!" Sakumat said. "But seeing how the meadow will grow slowly, perhaps I'll get used to it."

When the burban came to visit later on, the boy spoke to him for a long time about the new plan. His father said it was a wonderful idea.

"Not even the burban of Ankara has a meadow in his home!" he said.

Then Madurer fell asleep.

"My friend, how long will it take to paint the meadow the way he wishes?" the burban asked Sakumat.

"The way he wishes? At least four months, sire. Perhaps five."

"And this is the last room. Four months will be enough..." Ganuan said to himself.

"May I ask, sire, enough for what?"

"To expand my son's quarters. Seal off the

windows, knock down the walls of the nearby rooms. The meadow will not be disturbed. The entranceway could be in the room with the mountains. Nevertheless—" Suddenly confused, the burban looked at the painter. "Forgive me, my friend," he said. "I am speaking as though your body and your mind belonged to me."

Sakumat smiled. "My body and my mind are very much alive and in my possession, sire. There isn't a single moment of time spent in this home that I don't desire and cherish."

There was a brief silence.

"I have noticed, my friend, that ever since you joined us here—and it has been well over a year now—you have let your beard grow," the burban pointed out in a light tone. "When you arrived, you were little more than a smooth-faced young man. Now your beard makes you look more solemn. For how much longer will it grow? Are you not afraid your friends will be unable to recognize you when they see you again?"

"Sire, I'll tell them, 'Here I am! It's Sakumat! It's me, your friend! Do you like my long beard?' And my friends will like it. And perhaps the more playful of them will tug it affectionately."

Ganuan smiled. "Your heart is big, my friend and brother."

"Sire," Sakumat said with a bow, "as I've told you, I'm here out of my own joy."

On the walls of the third room the meadow was born, and it was a meadow in springtime. The grass sprang up, short and thick in a fragrant shade of green. The flowers had short stems and barely opened buds.

Madurer's condition improved day after day. Soon the boy could leave his bed to watch Sakumat working and hand the painter the brushes he needed, as he used to do. During the day, when he fell into one of his slumbers, he would awaken to

find little patches of taller grass and more developed flowers.

Then, butterflies began to appear. Madurer would look for different species illustrated in his books and would take them to Sakumat, who would paint them in the meadow. There were butterflies from all over the world among the flowers, but some of the butterflies, like many of the flowers, weren't to be found in any land or in any book.

"Can I help you paint, Sakumat?" the boy asked one day. "These yellow flowers look easy to do. Can I paint one too?"

Sakumat froze, one arm still raised, and hung his head.

"What's wrong, Sakumat?" Madurer asked, taking a little step back. "You don't want me to paint the yellow flower? It isn't very important. I don't want to ruin the meadow."

The painter slowly turned around. "Forgive me for not thinking of it myself," he said. "You'll paint the yellow flower, and other flowers too, if you like."

"No, I don't want to ruin the meadow, truly. I won't paint anything, because I don't know how to."

"You won't ruin the meadow, Madurer. It isn't difficult to paint the yellow flower. I'll help you. It won't be difficult."

"No. I'm afraid I'll do it wrong. I don't want to paint anymore."

Sakumat laid down his brush and stared at the meadow for a long time, as though nothing had happened. Then he motioned the boy closer. "Here's what we'll do," he said. "I'll teach you to paint the yellow flower on parchment. That way you can do it wrong and no harm will be done. Once your flowers are good, you'll help me paint the ones in the meadow."

And so, a little each day, Sakumat taught Madurer to paint flowers, and blades of grass. And, since flowers and butterflies aren't so different, butterflies too.

It took three weeks for Madurer to be satisfied with his skills and to begin to add tiny flowers and butterflies to the meadow, which had become a ripe field in June bursting with colourful life. By now, not a flower was missing in the thickness of the grass. Madurer's painting grew bolder with each passing day, blending in with Sakumat's, ruffling the order of the shapes, the composure of the greenery. It was as if a plump hare had hopped around from

place to place or had crouched to sniff out danger in the meadow. And the meadow drank in those differences like a real forest of grass and blossoms, warm and radiant beneath a sky without sorrow.

One day, Madurer began to add slender, golden stalks that rose through the grass, their tips peeking up ever so slightly into the blue of the sky.

"Has wheat arrived in our meadow?" asked a smiling Sakumat, who would stop from time to time behind the boy to watch his work. "Did the wind carry it all the way here from the mighty valley of Firat?"

"It isn't wheat," Madurer replied, very serious. "These aren't stalks of wheat."

"They aren't? But they look like wheat, though thinner..."

"Yes, they're a bit like wheat. But these are glowrushes."

"Glowrushes? That's a plant I've never heard of," Sakumat said, a curious look on his face. He leaned in closer to study one of the painted wisps more carefully.

"No one's ever heard of it," said Madurer. "It's a sort of firefly-plant."

"A firefly-plant?"

84

"Yes. On clear nights it lights up, you see. We don't see it glowing now, because it's daytime, but at night the glowrushes illuminate the meadow."

Sakumat made no reply, still studying the wisp.

That evening he spoke to the burban and asked that a man be sent to Malatya, to the merchant Kayaty's shop, which was in the square by the mosque.

A week later, in the middle of the night, Sakumat gently shook the sleeping boy's shoulder. In the darkness of the room, seated silently on a cushion a few paces away from the bed, was the burban.

"Wake up, Madurer."

"What? What is it, Sakumat?"

"Look."

Bewildered, the boy sat up in bed. All around him, in the darkness, hundreds of slender wisps glowed with a golden light. Bending this way and that, they shone throughout the dark meadow and seemed to sway in the wind.

"The glowrushes!" the boy cried, leaping to his feet on the bed, amazed.

"It's a clear night," Sakumat said.

Madurer looked overhead. Hundreds of specks of light shone through the darkness of the sky.

His face tilted straight up, his feet sinking into the cushions, Madurer turned around, gaping. He rapidly clenched and unclenched his hands before his chest, as if grasping at the air, and sighed. "Ooh! Does my father know?" he asked without looking down.

"Yes, Madurer. I am here," the burban said softly. He too, invisible on his cushion, sighed deeply. His breath, fuller and slower than Madurer's, was like the wave of wind bending the glowrushes.

12

The preparation of the new rooms was suspended.

Soon after the end of spring, Madurer had another attack, one worse than the last. For three days he remained unconscious, tormented and consumed with a violent fever. Four doctors were urgently summoned from nearby cities, and they remained at his bedside, conferring and watching over his suffering.

Even when the boy recovered and his long, peaceful naps during the day began again, the

doctors stayed on in Nactumal to continue their observations. They enquired constantly about his appetite, playfully asked him about any physical changes he might have felt and had him describe what he'd dreamed.

While the doctors examined Madurer, Sakumat would leave the palace and go on one of his rides around the valley, down the rugged paths and the rocky edges of the pastures. At times he would leave his horse grazing and stroll down the arid rows of stones, leaning over occasionally to brush his fingers against a sharp protrusion or feel the consistency of the white dust into which the rock crumbled to the touch.

The doctors departed after a week, taking their leave of the boy and the painter with silent bows.

When they were gone, the burban summoned Sakumat and said, "My friend, all hope is lost. Forced to speak sincerely, the doctors said my son will not live much longer. His body, forever a hesitant guest in this world, is soon to pass on. The blind, powerful force of life—the same that kept me from going deaf as they uttered the words, and now keeps me from losing my mind from this anguish—is abandoning his feeble flesh. My friend,

never have I known such great pain. Not even at the death of Aviget, the bride so dear to my heart. And yet, I wish it were even greater, as the one within me seems too small."

Ganuan hung his head and wept, and Sakumat wept with him.

Then the painter asked, "How much longer might he live, sire?"

"Not more than a year, they say."

"Do you wish me to leave?"

"I have no wishes, but that is the last thing I would wish for. Stay, if you can."

Sakumat went out riding again. His route broadened, following the road that cut sharply through the meagre fields and led just below the northern edge of the valley. From there, moving along its upper northern side, he made his way in and out of low groves of strong, spiny oaks, delving into steep tracts which his old horse faced very cautiously. Making a broad curve just before the mountains, the path then veered south, along the western side, crossing barely traced trails and the rugged tracks of herds and caravans. From any point along the journey, except the brief wooded patches, the burban's white palace could be seen, standing out

like a crown jewel amid the heap of stones on the valley floor.

Less direct than his ascent, his descent along the southern side crossed over terrain with coarse vegetation, spotted with patches of colourful flowers and bluish *cupatja* bushes. His course came to an end on a well-trodden path which—crossing the valley's richer pastures, where roaming sheep grazed calmly—led back to the first houses in the village.

Sakumat went on this entire journey three times, as though forgetting upon each return that he had completed it, paying no mind to the horse's increasingly weary pace. Then he led the animal to the stables and went back inside the palace, where utter silence reigned.

Madurer was still asleep. Ganuan was sitting, his eyes closed, at the boy's bedside.

Sakumat walked along the painted walls, staring at the mountains and the plain, the besieged city and the sea, the pirate ship and the lush meadow, in which the scattered glowrushes almost seemed to stand out more clearly than usual. Three times, slowly, as he'd done around the valley, he travelled through those lands and noticed things new to him,

shapes and events and colours he didn't remember creating.

With the first sign of Madurer's reawakening, the burban slipped away like a shadow.

"Good morning, Sakumat," said the boy.

"Good morning to you too, Madurer."

"I slept a long time, didn't I?"

"Yes, and you slept soundly. Are you all right now?"

"Yes, I'm fine. A little weak, like the other times."

"You'll stay in bed for a few days. I'll read you stories."

"Wonderful! And then we can start working again. I'll ask my father, the burban, to have the new rooms finished quickly. It shouldn't take much longer."

"No, not much longer. We're not done planning our new pictures, though, Madurer. I have some ideas, but I need to think it over carefully, like you did before deciding on the meadow, remember?"

"Yes."

"Meanwhile, until you're out of bed, we'll read stories and look at the pictures in your books."

"Will we make drawings on parchment too?"

"If it doesn't tire you too much. I'll teach you to paint birds."

But over the following days Madurer was still too weak to draw. Sakumat read him lots of stories, talking with him about the events and characters. As he did, he noticed how Madurer's strength was struggling, even more than the last time, to find its way back to the young boy's body.

But between one nap and the next, Madurer's thinking was quick and sharp. However, at times he was taken by a curious distraction, an absent-minded moment during which he would utter confused, sometimes even meaningless words. It was as though his mind was voicing them, unbound by language. His naps during the day also grew longer and more persistent.

"Building new rooms is a good idea," Sakumat said, "but I have a better one."

"Is that what you've been thinking about these days?"

"Yes. And as I thought about it, it became even more wonderful."

"Then tell me what it is, Sakumat."

"It's this: if we keep adding walls, we won't be able to look out over the whole landscape anymore.

I mean, it would become too big to really play with it. It would stay the same for a long time, and it would be less alive."

Madurer was quiet, listening carefully.

"Basically, I think these walls are all we need," Sakumat said.

"But they're full!" Madurer pointed out. "The *Tigrez* is big in the sea, and it couldn't get any bigger. The meadow's in full bloom. There are even the glowrushes that light up at night. What else could we paint?"

As he spoke, Sakumat played with the boy's hands, like he often did. "Remember how we painted those things, Madurer?" he asked, clasping his fingers a little tighter. "How tiny the ship was at first? And how 'unripe' the meadow was?"

"Yes. We made them little by little. Bit by bit."

"And remember something from even further back? That the world doesn't have gaps and doesn't stop?"

For a moment Madurer was quiet, weighing his smaller fingers in the painter's larger ones. "You mean our landscapes can keep going?"

"They can keep going, yes. And changing. If we want them to."

"Change how? By becoming more beautiful?"

"They're already beautiful, Madurer. But we can move forward in the story, add the rest of their lives."

The boy seemed exhausted. Sleep was overcoming him again. "Yes, let's do it that way," he said. "Later you can tell me how..."

Even for Sakumat it had been an exhausting conversation. He listened as the boy's troubled breathing fell into a steadier rhythm. Then he shut his eyes. Like from slashes in a tree branch, from his closed eyelids seeped glistening tears.

With the excuse of bringing news about the construction of the new rooms, the burban visited Madurer more often. "The work is going well, son. Soon they will be ready and—"

"Thank you, Father. But there isn't much of a hurry anymore."

"Why do you say that?"

"Because Sakumat and I have decided to continue working on our landscapes. We need to add the rest of their lives."

Without saying a word, the burban stared at his son.

"Maybe I'm not explaining myself well, my father," Madurer said, and took him by the hand. "I want to explain it to you from close up."

Ganuan followed his son until they were standing in front of the mountains in the first room.

"What do you see, Father?" Madurer asked, gesturing at part of the scene.

"The mountain. And on the side of it, Mutkul the shepherd's hut with the pen for his goats. Then I see—"

"One moment, Father. What you see, is it exactly what you've seen before?"

"Yes, I think so. No, wait... Am I wrong, or should Mutkul have more goats? There seem to be fewer of them."

"Well done!" Madurer cried. "There were once eighteen, to be precise!"

"And now there are nine," the burban said, counting. "Only nine."

"Yes, nine. Eight nannies and a ram. And do you know why?"

"Did a bear come one night, perhaps?"

"No, Father."

"Cattle thieves, then."

"No thieves. There are thieves, but they're on the other side of the mountain. They never come to this side."

"Then Mutkul sold the goats that are missing."

"Mutkul wouldn't sell them, Father. He doesn't need money, because he eats cheese and drinks milk and wears clothes made of goatskin. You're getting closer, though!"

"He gave them away, then?"

"Yes!" cried Madurer. "You see, Father, Mutkul couldn't look after such a large herd anymore. The years have passed, and he isn't as nimble or as strong as he used to be. He can't climb the rocks and chase after the young strays anymore."

The burban bowed his head, listening.

"And so, he gave them away!" Madurer went on. "He gave them to a young shepherd who lives just beyond that ridge, and is named Bubakr, and has red hair."

"But Mutkul had a lame dog to help him, did he not?" asked the burban.

"Oh, he died," Madurer said in a light voice. "He died months ago. That's another reason why Mutkul doesn't keep a large herd. He doesn't trust other dogs."

"Is Mutkul very old now?"

"Not very old, Father. But he's fairly old."

"Like me?"

"No. He's older than you. And he's very tired—that is, fairly tired." Madurer looked up and said solemnly, "Time passes for everyone, Father."

"Of course," Ganuan said, looking away from his son to study other parts of the landscape. "I see something else new, down there. I cannot recall there being snow on those mountaintops."

"You're right. Winter's on its way," Madurer continued. "The bears have already gone into the caves to sleep." With his hand, he showed his father the developments. He pointed out the colour of the woods, which were less green than before. Vast areas of it were shaded brownish yellow, and further below, patches of the grassy fields had been singed by the evening chill. "See the cave up there, below the rocks?"

"Yes. Is that also new?"

"It was hidden behind the trees before. And see the bear's big head?"

"This?"

"No, that's the rock. A little lower... There!"

"Ah, yes, this is the bear. You need to look carefully to spot him."

"He's the last bear to go into hibernation. He's eaten lots over the last two months: berries, nuts, honey, fruit and even ants!"

"Even ants?"

"Yes, Father. Bears eat everything."

"Then his belly must be full."

"It's this big!" Laughing, Madurer imitated the gluttonous bear's waddle. Then he sat down on the cushions and continued. "It's made him very groggy, you see? Now he's going into the cave to sleep all winter long."

"But for now he is still awake," the burban said, brushing his fingertips over the shadow of the bear inside the cave.

"He's not sleeping yet. Once in a while he crawls outside and munches on some plants. Only for the taste, though, because his tummy's already stuffed. He sniffs the air and smells winter. Then, pretty soon, he'll go back into his den and stay there for many months. But first he'll push a nice, big pile of dry branches in front of the opening to protect himself from the wind while he's sleeping."

The burban looked around, dazed. He said, "It is not cold in here, is it? Would you like me to have them light a fire?"

"No, Father. It's not cold," Madurer replied. "It isn't as warm as before, because summer's over, but there's no need for a fire."

The entire landscape in the first room had changed—not noticeably, but in its every detail. Instead of Talya's blue-curtained cart heading toward the plain, now there was a brown-curtained cart which a pair of oxen were pulling toward the mountain. No horse was tethered to the back of the cart, but two big, shaggy dogs trotted along by its wheels.

The city on the plain was no longer under siege. Around its walls, by its big, wide-open gates, tiny merchants' workshops could be seen. Now very small, beside a blue nomad tent, was Talya's cart and a tiny girl, almost invisible, practising acrobatics.

"How did the siege end, Madurer?"

The boy invited his father to sit down beside him. Then he began to tell the tale. "It ended in quite a strange and even funny way. First of all, the head of the besiegers, King Ras-Patay, grew ill from impatience after spending three years attacking the city—so ill that he died. Once he was dead there was no longer any reason to attack the city, so the troops were supposed to leave. But Prince Njulabey,

the son of the man who died, became king. The prince, remember? He's the one who sent a love letter by carrier pigeon to the besieged princess, whose name was Mutihah, and now that he was king, he didn't want to leave, because if he left he'd lose her. But he couldn't stay there without fighting either, without continuing the siege, because his generals would've been offended if he'd made them stand around twiddling their thumbs. So, what did Njulabey do? He met in secret with Princess Mutihah beneath a plum tree and they agreed to have a baby. The next day, the prince, who was now king, summoned his generals and said:

"'Who can prevent me from stepping down as king?'

"'No one, King Njulabey, but we need an heir to the throne!'

"'There is an heir.'

"'Where?'

"'He's in the warm, comfy belly of his mother, Princess Mutihah, who is as beautiful as the sun in May and my chosen bride. He'll come out in nine months' time, and do you think he'll be pleased, when he's born, to be born in a city besieged by his own generals?'

"And with this, my father, the generals were silenced and the siege was ended."

"A clever trick indeed." The burban smiled. "And then the boy was born? Or was it a girl?"

"A boy. There he is, up there!" Madurer said, pointing. "You see, up in the city's tallest tower? His name is Nakutad."

"He is already a grown boy, though."

"Of course. He was born over ten years ago. He has a telescope, see? That's to watch the stars with."

"Oh, yes, I see. But where are the stars?"

Madurer raised a finger to his lips, as though revealing a secret. "Soon Sakumat will paint the night, Father, like he did over the meadow," he said eagerly. "The sun, down there, is setting now. Then we'll make the darkness, slowly but surely, and then the stars. That way the little king can gaze at them. He can gaze at them as long as he likes, even until morning, because he's a king and no one can send him to bed."

"Where is the ship going, Sakumat?" Madurer asked with a faint voice.

By now he was spending much of the day on the cushions, watching the painter work. He hadn't suffered any other attacks, but his strength hadn't returned. In fact, once it had reached a certain point, it began to fade. Slowly the boy was growing pale, and his breathing more troubled.

"Remember when I asked you where Talya's cart was heading, Madurer?" the painter asked. "Remember what you told me?"

"I told you, *It's going far, far away, Sakumat.*"

"The ship is going far, far away too."

"But then, Sakumat, you asked me, *Is it going toward the hill or toward the plain?*"

"At sea, there's only the horizon, Madurer."

"Then the ship is going toward the horizon," said the boy. He stared intently at the vessel, which, tilted slightly to the left, was now far off at sea, its billowing sails tinged pink.

"After that horizon, there's another horizon," Sakumat said. He was painting with his back to the boy, using his brush to touch up the small, frothy waves at the sides of the brig.

"We can't see the horizon that comes after," the boy observed.

"But it's there."

"Can Madurer see it?"

"What's that?" Sakumat asked, looking over his shoulder.

"Madurer, the cabin boy, the one who's at the very front of the ship," the boy repeated, a bit louder. "He can see the next horizon, can't he?"

"Of course. He sees it. He sees all the horizons, and he's the first to see them."

Madurer's naps lasted more than half his days and all night long. They were slightly restless, but without suffering. It was as though in his sleep the boy was trying to explain something to someone, or to himself, yet never fully managed to. When he awoke, he never realized he'd slept for long.

"The *Tigrez* is so far away! If we didn't know it was the *Tigrez*, we wouldn't be able to recognize it!" he said once, upon waking.

"It is the *Tigrez*, though. See the sails? Only the *Tigrez* has sails like this, in all the sea between Greece and Egypt."

"What horizon is Madurer seeing now?"

"A horizon just like the one we're looking at, probably," Sakumat said. "The sea is very big. In it are many horizons."

"But after the last horizon, what will Madurer see?"

"There is no last horizon," Sakumat said. "The world is round. The horizon never ends."

"So when the *Tigrez* is gone—I mean, when we can't see it anymore—it'll sail around the other side of the horizon, until it comes back!" the boy exclaimed weakly.

"Of course. One day or the other, his horizon will be... that." Sakumat pointed his blue-tipped paintbrush at the other side of the room, where the sea stretched out in an unbroken line.

With some difficulty, joyfully, Madurer shifted on the cushions to have a better view of the sea on that side. "It's true!" he said, straining his voice. "Once it's gone all the way around, we'll see it arrive on the other side! And it'll be a tiny dot again, remember?"

Sakumat put down his paintbrush and went to sit beside the boy. "Yes. When we see it appear, we'll need to be patient, because the dot might be a different ship. The *Tigrez* isn't the only one sailing the world's seas."

They laughed softly, staring at the open sea together.

"Of course, the *Tigrez* isn't the only one," Madurer said, "but even if it isn't the right dot, sooner or later the *Tigrez* will turn up."

"It certainly will," Sakumat replied. "Who could ever stop the *Tigrez*?"

The boy turned back to look at the wall on which the ship, now tiny, was sailing toward the first horizon. "I hope it's very fast," he said. "That it quickly arrives at... at... That it soon finds its horizons."

Sakumat looked at him. "You've said a beautiful thing, Madurer."

"What did I say?"

"That the *Tigrez* is going off to find its horizons. That's poetic."

"Then I'm a poet, Sakumat!"

The painter lowered his head in agreement. "And quite a good one, I'd say."

Madurer laughed. Then he turned toward his friend, concerned. "Your face looks tired, Sakumat," he said seriously. "You're very pale, and a bit thin too."

"Am I truly pale and thin, Madurer? I should go look at myself in the mirror... Actually, maybe I'd better not. I wouldn't want to frighten myself. Let's leave the fright inside the mirror."

"Yes, your reflection is in there, waiting to frighten you, but don't you go!" the boy exclaimed. Then he added, calmly, "Maybe you're tired because I can't help you paint anymore."

"I don't think so, Madurer," the painter said. "Working with a brush isn't tiring. Besides, the ship is sailing so fast that soon all it will take are a few dabs of paint."

Madurer turned his gaze back to the empty sea to his right. He was quiet for several minutes,

breathing slowly and thinking. Then he closed his eyes and, for a moment, fell asleep.

Sakumat ran his hands over his face in silence. His beard was long now, and time had marked it with white, wavy strands.

The boy opened his eyes. "What if, on the other side of the world, between one horizon and the next, someone sinks the *Tigrez*?" he asked with a frown, as though during that moment he'd had an ominous dream.

"That could happen, Madurer," Sakumat said slowly, pulling his hands away from his face. "Old Krapulos is certainly a fine captain, the crew is alert and reliable, the ship is sturdy... But it could happen. Do you think it will happen?"

"No. But they'll try!" Madurer said almost angrily.

"Who will try?"

"The Spaniards. And the Greeks too."

"All at once? Oh, the poor *Tigrez*..."

"Not all at once. First the Spaniards, off the shores of Libya, and almost a month later, the Greeks."

"But Krapulos himself is Greek! Why do they chase him down? Are they also pirates?"

"Don't you remember what that boy said in the story about Zineb and the pirates, Sakumat? He said, *All pirates are everyone's enemies.*"

"No, he said, *For a pirate, the whole world's a pirate.*"

"That's more or less the same thing, isn't it?"

"Yes, you're right. Then what's going to happen?"

"Well, the Spaniards are going to sink in a jiffy, because they'll be battling while drunk on wine."

"Praise be to Allah, and His Prophet. What about the Greeks?"

"With the Greeks it'll be harder. The *Tigrez* is going to be broadsided."

"Victims aboard?"

"Purtik, the boatswain. Off with his head, from a cannonball."

"Well, he was a renegade. Sooner or later he was bound to lose his head. He leaves behind a widow in Rhodes, if I remember correctly... But she's already been remarried for twenty-three years now."

Madurer laughed feebly. "But you know who's going to make the *Tigrez* win?" he said.

"Who?"

"Madurer."

"And how does he do that? He's only a cabin boy."

"Yes, but at some point during the battle against the Greeks, somebody's got to dash across the yard to adjust the square-sail, and while under fire from the Greeks nobody else can do it. Seven of them try, and they drop like flies, and some crash down onto the deck, and some end up overboard."

"Poor souls! So Madurer goes up?"

"Yes, he scampers up like a cat."

"But don't the Greeks fire at him too? Or are they drunk on Greek wine?"

"No, they fire, and aim true. But Madurer's no fool. As he climbs, he stays hidden behind the mast and moves so quickly that no one can get him in their sights. Besides, the sea is choppy and everything is swaying."

"Good. So he manages to set the square-sail..."

"Then the *Tigrez* veers around and rams the Greeks' ship. Almost all of them die, because there are sharks in the water. Three survive and become pirates."

"Oh, poor Krapulos! Three extra mouths to feed!"

"Two more, Sakumat. Purtik lost his head, so his mouth to feed is gone."

"What about the ones who tried to climb the rigging? The ones who fell, wherever they ended up?"

"Oh, right. They... Two of them died. One from the sharks and one when he crashed onto the deck. Two of the seven died. This way, there isn't a single extra mouth to feed!"

"And who were they?"

"No one really important. In fact, not important at all. No one even knows what their names were. To remember their names, we'd have to go through those of all the others. Basically, they didn't really exist much even before, understand?"

"Like the green butterfly on the green moss."

Madurer laughed.

"So the *Tigrez* does well out of this, with two new pirates!" said Sakumat.

"Of course!" said Madurer. "Because they'll be perfectly loyal to Krapulos. They're from the isle of Salamis, just like he is. In fact, one of them is his cousin."

"What a small world!" Sakumat said, shrugging his shoulders. "Well, then, will there be a reward for our cabin boy?"

"He'll be made boatswain."

"So quickly? Isn't he a bit too young? And aren't the other pirates jealous?"

"No, none of them are jealous. None of them want to be boatswain anyway. They don't want the responsibility. But since a boatswain is needed... Besides, when the battle happens, we can have Madurer already be sixteen. You can be boatswain at sixteen, right?"

"Aboard the *Tigrez*, yes," Sakumat said. "But you're tired now, Madurer. You should—"

Madurer cut him off with a wave of his hand. "All those battles will slow down their voyage a bit, though!"

"A bit, yes. But there will be a strong wind. All the wind they need."

"Maybe it's better if there wasn't the battle against the Spaniards. Let's change it: that battle never happened."

"If the Spaniards only knew, just think how they would celebrate!" Sakumat said. "But now, Madurer, rest."

The boy lay down among the cushions. "When the *Tigrez* returns and it's close up, will it be clear that Madurer's the boatswain?"

"It will definitely be clear. And by then, perhaps

he'll already have become captain. A captain can be seen from far away, can't he?"

That game was the last one Madurer played with vigour.

"See that, Father? The meadow is falling asleep," Madurer said.

Nine months had gone by since the fateful attack. The boy now lay in the third room, on a bed that was light, easier to move around. He no longer left it, and the burban came to visit him frequently, at times spending the entire day at his son's side.

Around them, Sakumat had slowly darkened the meadow's summer tones. The lush grass had

changed colour; one by one the flowers had curled and withered, and had then begun to droop. Like the slow wave of time, the brush passed over the grass again and again, instilling it with a dusky light.

"The meadow is falling asleep," Madurer repeated, his voice so faint it could barely be heard.

As Sakumat slowly made his way along the walls, the little bed was moved so the boy could watch his work. Large cushions propped up his head, even as he slept, to make it easier for him to breathe. The boy often repeated his words several times, as though instantly forgetting he'd said them.

"The meadow is falling asleep, Father."

"Yes, Madurer," the burban said. "Are the insects falling asleep as well?"

"Some of them. Some of the insects are falling asleep, because they have short lives. They couldn't keep their wings beautiful during the winter. They couldn't keep them beautiful, so they gave them to the meadow."

"Yes, how right you are," Ganuan said. "In the whole meadow I cannot see a single butterfly."

"You know how the meadow feels?" The boy's eyesight had also grown weak. Madurer often asked

that his bed be moved closer to one spot or another beside the walls so he could see the transformation more clearly. "Father, do you know how the meadow feels?"

"The grass, you mean?"

"Yes, the grass, the flowers. Even the things that aren't grass and flowers. The earth, the animals, the pebbles, the roots... The meadow. The whole meadow. You know how it feels?"

"How does it feel?" Ganuan leaned his head closer to his son's.

"The meadow feels happily tired," the boy said with the tone of someone revealing a secret, "like when you've run a lot when playing. The meadow has run a lot..."

All at once he fell silent.

The burban sat there quietly, his head still very close, and waited.

"The meadow has run a lot," Madurer said, "with the insects and the seeds and the wind. Even its colours have gone far away. Gone and returned many times. And then—"

He nodded off suddenly, abruptly, which was happening to him more and more often. The burban raised his head, then sat up straight. In silence he

watched the subtle movement of Sakumat's shoulders as the man painted.

The boy slept only briefly. He woke without stirring and began to speak again as though rather than falling asleep, he'd only paused to catch his breath. "The meadow doesn't feel above and below," he said.

"What do you mean, Madurer?" the burban asked, leaning over again.

"It doesn't feel its roots in the earth and its stalks in the air," Madurer said. "It doesn't feel inside and outside. Understand?"

The burban was silent.

"Look, Father," the boy said, pointing all around. "You see, the meadow's roots are in the sky of the earth, and the flowers are roots in the air." With his open hand, from a distance he covered the painted strip on the wall. "The flowers are roots in the air. The animals come in and go out, they're inside and outside. They go into the earth, they come out from the sky. The meadow protects them as they pass through. It protects them. It feels them all and protects them."

Ganuan lifted one of his son's hands and kissed it. "What Sakumat says is true, my son. You are a poet."

Madurer smiled. "The meadow is a poet," he said, and again he nodded off.

Sakumat had once more come full circle. He changed paints and brushes, and began to go back over the meadow like a new wave of time. He added space between one stem and the other. Many stems he severed. The flowers crumbled to dust and the brown carpet of earth showed through the last remaining grass.

Ganuan didn't speak to the painter, nor did the painter speak to him. When the father would enter his son's room, the two men would greet each other with a little bow. At times, when the child was sleeping, Sakumat would go out, though without leaving the palace. Then he would return and silently resume his work. Madurer's few needs were now seen to only by the elderly Alika, helped by the painter and the burban himself.

"Do you want to talk with me some more, Father?" Madurer asked.

"If you like."

The boy looked at him, almost with curiosity. After a moment of silence he said, "I love you very much, Father."

"I love you too, Madurer."

"I love Sakumat very much."

"I love him too," Ganuan said, and he smiled.

Madurer smiled as well. "He's very good, isn't he?" he asked.

"He might be the best in the world," his father replied.

"I think this meadow is his finest work," Madurer said, knitting his brow slightly.

"Even finer than the mountains, and the sea?"

"Yes. It's even finer."

"You are an expert now, so it must be true."

They spoke very softly, in the softest whisper the boy could manage, so the painter wouldn't hear. They shared a few more words, then were quiet for a long moment.

"Are the glowrushes falling asleep too, Madurer?" the burban asked, his voice very low.

"Yes, of course. The whole meadow is falling asleep, you see. It's waking into sleep, because when you're awake, isn't it like the dream of someone who's sleeping?"

"On winter nights, the light of the glowrushes will be gone?" Ganuan asked, looking around at the darkened meadow.

"But the stars will be there, Father," Madurer said.

Ganuan hung his head. He stared at his hands that lay on his lap as though they were two animals he'd killed without meaning to. Then he said gently, "The stars are far away. The glowrushes are close by."

"Really, Father?" Madurer asked, raising his head toward him slightly. "Don't you know they're the same thing? Don't—"

Ganuan looked at his son, who had fallen silent and was resting his head, his breathing slow and raspy from the effort of speaking. "They are the same thing?" the burban asked.

"Yes, Father. The same."

16

When Madurer had died and the household and the village had wept for many days, the burban summoned Sakumat.

"You are my brother now," he said. "My home is your home, and the home of your heirs. If you do not wish to remain in your home, you will take with you half my riches in gold, gems, spices and precious silks."

The painter bowed. His beard was almost completely white now. The last months spent in

Madurer's quarters had also whitened his skin and drawn fine wrinkles at the corners of his eyes. "I have already had half your riches, sire," he said, "and yet the word 'brother' is sweet to my ears. I ask you only for a young horse. Mine was already old when I arrived. It wouldn't withstand the journey through the mountains."

Many were the words the burban uttered, urging Sakumat to accept gifts and riches, but without success.

Days later, on a fresh white horse, the painter, of his own accord, left the palace and the village. At the mouth of the valley, before Nactumal disappeared from sight, he stopped the horse, gathered a bundle of brushwood, placed the case containing his paintbrushes on top, and set fire to it. He sat there, watching as the smoke from the wood disappeared among the greyish rocks and the flames of the little blaze flickered in unusual shades.

When it had all turned to ash, Sakumat looked at Nactumal for the last time and got back on the horse.

In Malatya, two days later, they barely recognized him. Many asked what had kept him away. Sakumat told everyone it had been a long job, and said nothing more.

Once news of his return had spread, people began to knock on his door, asking him to paint scenes of hunting and fountains, of birds and flowers. After saying no to the tenth person who'd come, and for the tenth time refusing to explain the reason, Sakumat sold his house and bade his friends farewell forever.

"You were gone for such a long time, and already you're leaving?"

Smiling, he hugged them each in silence.

Then he set off and rode for three weeks, over the mountains, along the Ceyhan River, past Adana, and Içel, beyond the mouth of the turbulent Göksu River, along the coast. Farther on, at the edge of a little village scattered amid boulders as big as elephants, he bought a little house that looked like one of the many rocks, a very short distance to the beach.

From there he could hear the sound of the waves, constantly, yet like a silence.

He met the people from the village and made a few friends, with whom he would drink tea, cook meals and talk tranquilly of things present.

He lived a long, peaceful life as a fisherman.

## AVAILABLE AND COMING SOON
## FROM PUSHKIN CHILDREN'S BOOKS

We created Pushkin Children's Books to share tales from different languages and cultures with younger readers, and to open the door to the wide, colourful worlds these stories offer.

From picture books and adventure stories to fairy tales and classics, and from fifty-year-old bestsellers to current huge successes abroad, the books on the Pushkin Children's list reflect the very best stories from around the world, for our most discerning readers of all: children.

**THE MURDERER'S APE**
**SALLY JONES AND THE FALSE ROSE**
**THE LEGEND OF SALLY JONES**

*Jakob Wegelius*

**WHEN LIFE GIVES YOU MANGOES**
**IF YOU READ THIS**

*Kereen Getten*

**BOY 87**
**LOST**
**MELT**
**FAKE**

*Ele Fountain*

**THE LETTER FOR THE KING**
**THE SECRETS OF THE WILD WOOD**
**THE SONG OF SEVEN**
**THE GOLDSMITH AND THE MASTER THIEF**

*Tonke Dragt*


**HOW TO BE BRAVE**
**HOW TO BE TRUE**

*Daisy May Johnson*


**THE MYSTERY OF THE MISSING MUM**

*Frances Moloney*


**LAMPIE**

*Annet Schaap*


**THE MISSING BARBEGAZZI**
**THE HUNGRY GHOST**

*H.S. Norup*


**SCHOOL FOR NOBODIES**
**THE THREE IMPOSSIBLES**
**THE DANGEROUS LIFE OF OPHELIA BOTTOM**

*Susie Bower*


**THE ELEPHANT**
**MY BROTHER BEN**

*Peter Carnavas*


**LENNY'S BOOK OF EVERYTHING**
**DRAGON SKIN**

*Karen Foxlee*